CARRIMEBAC
The Town That Walked

David Barclay Moore

illustrated by
John Holyfield

Candlewick Press

ALL THE FOLKS in Walkerton, Georgia, remembered the hot, sweaty afternoon when ol' Rootilla Redgums and her peculiar grandson strolled into town.

Aunt Minnie's cat hisssked. Uncle Jo's dog snargggled. And all
of Peat Slewfoot's pet crows suddenly flew south for the winter.
Only it wasn't near winter yet. It was only ol' Rootilla Redgums.

Some said she was older than dirt—Georgia's bright-red dirt.
Others said she was older than Canoochee Creek, which ran
straight through Liberty County.

If you asked ol' Rootilla, she would say that she had been born in Africa in the year 1776—the same year the United States was born. She claimed to be almost one hundred years old.

Her grandson, Julius Jefferson, was only nine. But many people saw an older twinkle behind the boy's dark-brown eyes—if you happened to stare into them the right kind of way.

Soon after moving to Walkerton, Grandboy Julius found
a scrawny white duck wandering about its outskirts.

Right off, he fell in love with that duck and
named it Woodrow, or Woody for short.

Sometimes, one of the hungrier Walkerton villagers would snatch poor Woody and toss the bird into a boiling pot to cook for their supper. But after a while, when they peeked under the hot pot's lid, Woody would have vanished!

Mysteriously, the duck would pop up again
in Julius's caring arms.

Before Rootilla, Grandboy Julius, and Woodrow came
to town, the Black townsfolk's lives had been miserable.
They were always sad. The white towns surrounding
Walkerton had refused to buy any goods or crops from
them because of the color of the villagers' skin.

But after Rootilla came to town, Walkerton began to blossom.
All the other towns wanted to buy the things Rootilla had shown
the Walkerton Blacks how to make.

She taught them to weave rugs that never wore down, to fire or bake ceramic jugs that never emptied of sarsaparilla, and to carve wooden walking sticks that somehow never got you lost in the woods.

Most folks loved buying these wonderful handiworks.
But some who lived around Walkerton grew afraid.
They believed the Blacks who lived there practiced magic.

Rootilla always used to say that she wasn't magic.
But the things she made were . . .

ONE DAY Julius was skipping rocks across Canoochee Creek when one of those Fearful Folks accused him of stealing his duck.

"No, sir. Woody is my duck," said Julius. "I owned him since Granny and me came to Walkerton, almost a year ago."

"Liar!" the Fearful Man yelled. "By criminy, gimme back my dang duck right now, boy, or all of Walkerton will suffer darnation!"

Julius grabbed Woody and ran back into town.

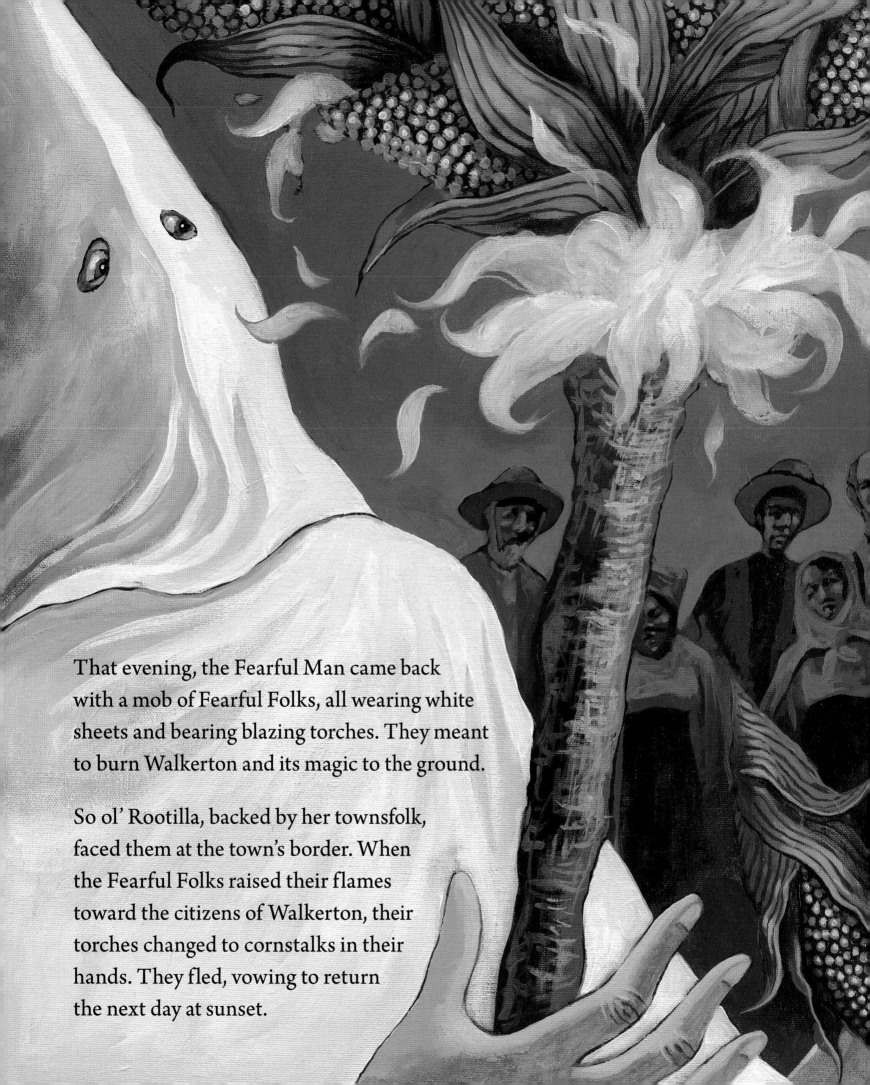

That evening, the Fearful Man came back
with a mob of Fearful Folks, all wearing white
sheets and bearing blazing torches. They meant
to burn Walkerton and its magic to the ground.

So ol' Rootilla, backed by her townsfolk,
faced them at the town's border. When
the Fearful Folks raised their flames
toward the citizens of Walkerton, their
torches changed to cornstalks in their
hands. They fled, vowing to return
the next day at sunset.

That same night Rootilla grew very sick.

In her little bed in their tiny house, she told Julius, "Dear young grandbaby of ten, this is my birthday. I am one hundred today, my last night with you. Once I leave, carry me back to where I was born, where from all of us come. Back home."

And with a smile, ol' Rootilla Redgums passed on.

All the next morning and all the next afternoon Julius spent carving, carving, carving.

It was almost sunset, but not quite, when the boy finally finished whittling the large log he had found. He had whittled it down into a curvy wooden pole.

The Walkerton folks planted the pole into the red dirt
at the border of town so that it stood there like a signpost.
They had each etched their names into this new post.
At its top, Julius had carved the word *CARRIMEBAC*.

Just before sunset, the Fearful Folks returned in greater numbers. They now toted more torches and even more scary things.

Brave and bold, little Julius Jefferson, backed by his townsfolk,
tied a slender rope around the fancy Carrimebac signpost.
The other end of the rope he looped around Woody
the duck's narrow ivory neck.

Julius pointed at Woody and shouted, "Now, duck! Walk!"

And the little duck strained, wobbled, and actually walked.
Pulling the entire small village slowly behind it.

The Fearful Folks stood frozen in astonishment. Most of
them dropped their torches and bolted toward home.

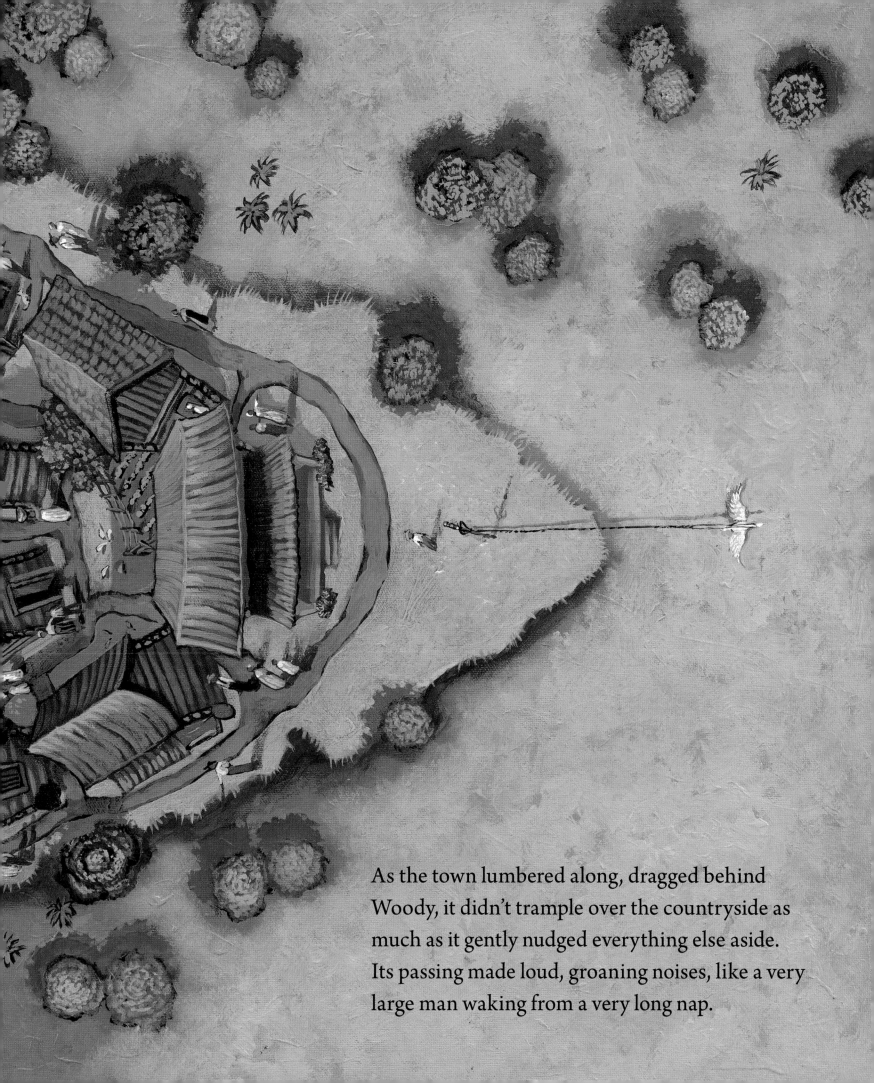

As the town lumbered along, dragged behind Woody, it didn't trample over the countryside as much as it gently nudged everything else aside. Its passing made loud, groaning noises, like a very large man waking from a very long nap.

It began to pick up speed. As the town sped across
Liberty County, it gathered a few more passengers.
Some Free Folk who spotted the town whisking by
happily leapt aboard, the way you might leap onto a
log swiftly floating down a stream. Still many other
gawkers were too afraid to take a chance and jump.

The Town That Walked sailed across Blackbeard Creek and the salt marshes. Woody's small webbed feet flew through the sticky mud and reeds as if they weren't even there.

Soon, the hamlet reached the ocean. In familiar
territory, Woody began to paddle furiously,
still hauling the entire village.

WHERE THE TOWN ONCE SAT, there now rests a natural lake. The locals named it Lake Carrimebac in honor of its former residents. No one in Liberty County, Georgia, ever heard anything about the town of Carrimebac ever again.

But we all know the stories about what happened after it sailed across the ocean. You don't? Well, some other time, perhaps . . .

In loving memory of my Bramer, Lenora Madeline Bolton,
who loved good books and good stories.

With thanks to Carlos Sirah, Asari Beale, Liz Bicknell, and Steven Malk.
DBM

To all of my North Carolina family.
Thank you for the love and support.
JH

First edition 2022

Library of Congress Catalog Card Number pending
ISBN 978-1-5362-1369-0

21 22 23 24 25 26 APS 10 9 8 7 6 5 4 3 2 1

Printed in Humen, Dongguan, China

This book was typeset in Arno.
The illustrations were done in acrylic.

Candlewick Press
99 Dover Street
Somerville, Massachusetts 02144

www.candlewick.com